DANIEL DEFOE

ROBINSON CRUSOE

CAMPFIRE™

KALYANI NAVYUG MEDIA PVT LTD
New Delhi

Sitting around the Campfire, telling the story, were:

Wordsmith	:	Dan Johnson
Illustrator	:	Naresh Kumar
Illustrations Editor	:	Jayshree Das
Colourist	:	Anil CK
Colour Consultant	:	RC Prakash
Letterer	:	Bhavnath Chaudhary
Editors	:	Eman Chowdhary
		Andrew Dodd

Cover Artists:

Illustrator	:	Suresh Digwal
Colourist	:	Rajeev Chauhan
Designer	:	Manishi Varshney

Published by Kalyani Navyug Media Pvt Ltd
101 C, Shiv House, Hari Nagar Ashram
New Delhi 110014
India
www.campfire.co.in

ISBN: 978-81-906963-1-9

Printed in India at Rave India

About The Author

Daniel Defoe was born in 1660 in St Giles, London. He is most well known for his critically acclaimed novel, *Robinson Crusoe*. When published in 1719, it was instantly met with great praise. This was largely because it was a groundbreaking work – no one had produced anything like this before, and some even claim it was the first novel in English.

After finishing his schooling, Defoe was sent to Morton's Academy at Stoke Newington – an educational institute for non-conformist Christians. In 1684, he married Mary Tuffley, and had eight children in the years that followed.

Defoe faced many trials and tribulations during his life. He tried his hand in business, as well as secretarial work, but neither of these occupations worked well for him. His monetary problems are well documented – he went bankrupt in 1692 – and in 1703, he was imprisoned for publishing pamphlets in support of the non-conformists.

In addition to novels and pamphlets, Defoe wrote biographies, guidebooks, journals, poems, and newspapers. In total, more than five hundred works have been attributed to his fertile mind. By far his most famous work, *Robinson Crusoe* was probably inspired by the true story of Alexander Selkirk and his experiences. Although it was not intended to be a work of fiction initially, it ended up as an adventure story, appealing to people of all ages and from all walks of life. Defoe's writing style is serious and factual, and the images he conjures up with his use of words, are vivid and realistic.

Towards the latter half of his life, he wrote under the name of Andrew Moreton, and was in hiding from his creditors when he died on 26th April 1731.

Robinson Crusoe

Friday

Young
Robinson Crusoe

Xury

Work with all your might, boys! Work faster!

It will be of no use! The ship will soon fill with water and sink.

The sea went as high as mountains, and broke upon us every three or four minutes.

The captain had started firing the guns as a distress signal. Soon, a lightship, which had survived the storm just ahead of us, sent a boat out to help us.

With great difficulty we all got safely to shore and walked on foot to Yarmouth.

If I had gone back to Hull then, I would have been happy. But my ill fate pushed me on with an obstinacy that nothing could resist.

My friend, the master's son, who had helped me before, was a changed man. His tone was altered. Looking very sad, he told his father who I was, and how I had only come on this voyage for a trial in order to travel further.

9

10

But my happiness was short-lived. My friend died soon after our arrival home. He had taught me many of the things that a sailor must know and I owed a great deal to him.

I resolved to go on the same voyage again. Soon I set out on the same vessel with the man who was my friend's mate in the previous voyage.

But before returning to Guinea, I visited my friend's widow and gave her two hundred pounds to keep for me.

I fell into terrible misfortunes on this second voyage. It began as our ship was making her course towards the Canary Islands.

Early in the morning one day, we were surprised by a Turkish rover from Sallee.

KA-BAM

KA-BAM

THWAK

We moved away as fast as our sails would carry us, but the rover continued to follow us and come close.

So, we prepared to fight.

OOOOOMPH!

But our ship was soon disabled and, with three of our men killed and eight wounded, we had to surrender.

Soon we were carried as prisoners into Sallee.

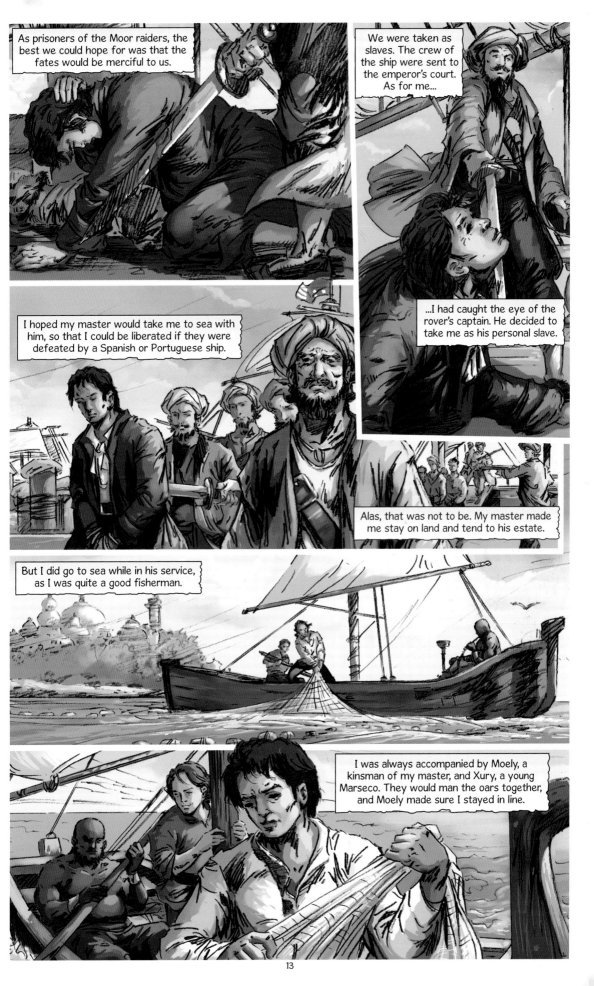

As prisoners of the Moor raiders, the best we could hope for was that the fates would be merciful to us.

We were taken as slaves. The crew of the ship were sent to the emperor's court. As for me...

...I had caught the eye of the rover's captain. He decided to take me as his personal slave.

I hoped my master would take me to sea with him, so that I could be liberated if they were defeated by a Spanish or Portuguese ship.

Alas, that was not to be. My master made me stay on land and tend to his estate.

But I did go to sea while in his service, as I was quite a good fisherman.

I was always accompanied by Moely, a kinsman of my master, and Xury, a young Marseco. They would man the oars together, and Moely made sure I stayed in line.

After two years into my forced servitude, an opportunity for freedom presented itself. My master had recently fitted the boat with a small stateroom and stocked it with supplies in case of emergency.

I must prepare for my celebration this evening! Take the boat out and bring me a great haul of fish that will please my guests!

As you wish, master.

I set my plan into motion and made sure we caught nothing.

There are no fish here either, Moely! We need to go further into the sea, if we want to catch anything today!

After all, we cannot dare to return to the master empty-handed.

It is time to execute my plan.

AAAHHH

I took Moely by surprise and tossed him overboard into the sea.

I have not hurt you, Moely! You swim well and the sea is calm. Make your way to shore, and I will do you no harm.

But if you come near the boat, I will shoot you through the head!

Then I turned towards Xury...

I – I swear I always be loyal! Where you go, I go as friend and companion!

Xury, if you are faithful to me, I will make you a great man, but if you will not agree to be true to me, I will throw you in the sea too.

The boy smiled and spoke so innocently that I could not distrust him.

After five days on the water, we were out of the reach of the Moors, but also out of fresh water. We pulled into a creek and found dry land.

GRRRR

Xury went to shore to find us fresh water. I was concerned he might be seen and attacked by one of the animals, or worse yet...

...wild men.

Robinson! Look! I have water and food!

15

One day, while we were travelling along the coast of Morocco, we spotted a great monster.

KA-POW

What kind of beast is that?

I have no idea, Xury. But I trust it can be killed like any other animal!

Robinson! The animal's flesh is not fit to eat!

And I wasted three bullets killing it!

Let me catch a quick nap, Xury. Then I will man the oars for a while.

His flesh might not be fit to eat, but his skin will be of some value to us.

We sailed on for ten more days, hoping to see a ship from a civilised nation.

16

Ten days later, we began to see inhabited land; and in two or three places, as we sailed by, we saw people standing upon the shore looking at us.

Xury, we should go to shore to greet these people.

No, Robinson! They wild men! Could be much danger!

I convinced Xury to accompany me. We kept at a distance, and talked with them by signs. I made signs for something to eat.

The natives understood and brought two pieces of dry flesh and corn.

We made signs of thanks to them, as we had nothing else to repay them with.

Then, at that very instant, two big cats came out of hiding and a wonderful opportunity presented itself to thank them.

KA-POW

I shudder to think what those giant cats would have done to these helpless natives. I dropped one cat with one shot, and the noise from my musket was enough to scare the other off.

It is impossible to express how astonished those poor creatures were at the noise of my gun. Some of them were so frightened that they fell down as if dead with terror.

Soon, Xury and I said bye to the friendly natives and left with enough provisions to last for days.

Eleven days later, near the Cape Verde Islands, we saw a ship.

Robinson! A ship with a sail! We are lost! The master sent a ship to find us!

No, Xury. Praise be to God, that ship is flying the flag of Portugal. At last, we are saved!

I observed the course the ship steered. I was soon convinced they were bound some other way, and did not intend to come any nearer to us.

I started rowing towards them determined to speak with them.

This kind of work does not suit me. It is contrary to the life I delighted in. I had not left my father's house, and ignored all his good advice to lead such a life...

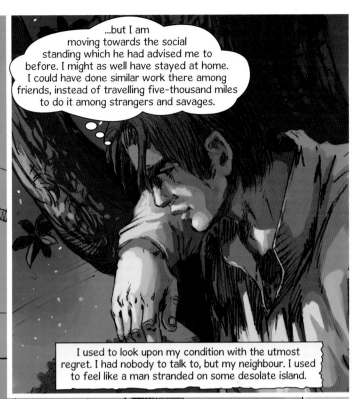

...but I am moving towards the social standing which he had advised me to before. I might as well have stayed at home. I could have done similar work there among friends, instead of travelling five-thousand miles to do it among strangers and savages.

I used to look upon my condition with the utmost regret. I had nobody to talk to, but my neighbour. I used to feel like a man stranded on some desolate island.

But there were some men who took great interest in me...

Robinson, we have been talking, and we have a business proposal for you. You know the Guinea coast. Would you like to go there on our behalf?

For what purpose, gentlemen?

Slaves, Robinson! We want you to go and get slaves to work on our estates.

One day the ship struck sand, and stopped moving. Soon after, the sea broke over us in such a manner that we expected to perish immediately.

We flung a lifeboat over the ship's side and jumped in it, leaving ourselves to God's mercy and the wild sea.

We had barely managed to travel some distance when a raging wave took us with great fury. Our boat toppled and we were all swallowed up in a moment.

SPAZOOSH!

Nothing can describe how confused I felt when I sank into the water. Though I swam very well, I was not able to escape the waves in order to breathe...

...until a wave carried me towards the shore...

...and left me half dead on the land.

One day, I went to get some corn for my meal and saw that the bag was almost empty.

There is no corn to go with our fowl. Must be the rats. I hope they get a right good bellyache from their gluttony!

Still, I can get some use from the bag.

Thinking that, I shook the dust from the bag, and took it home to put to other uses.

Little did I know at the time that the dust I shook from the bag would prove to be a blessing before long.

I had started thinking that God had no mercy left for me.

But then I discovered the first few stalks of corn.

I am ashamed, Heavenly Father. I throw your gift away without care and still you send me a miracle.

Truly, at times like that, I felt the loving hand of the Lord.

At other times, I felt the hand of God more fiercely.

What? An earthquake!

RMMMMMMBBBBL

RUFF RUFF

I was confused and the horror of dying in such a miserable condition caused great anguish in my mind. I did not know what I was saying.

Lord! What a miserable creature I am! I will certainly die for want of help!

Then tears rolled down my cheeks, and I could say no more for a good while.

What will become of me?

As I slept, I was plagued by terrible nightmares. The last eight years, since I had left my parents' house in Hull, had seen me living a wicked life. My sins visited me while I slept and, at last, the truth was revealed to me.

When I awoke, I went out to find food, but was too weak to hunt.

Just then, the answer I desired most came to me.

'...Call on me in the day of trouble, and I will deliver, and thou shalt glorify me...'

And I knew God had not forsaken me.

Having regained strength of body and peace of mind, I decided to explore my island further. I had been there for ten months and I wished to know my home better.

I made my way up the creek where I first came ashore, and was pleased to see tobacco growing wild on the bank. A little further down, I found wild sugar cane and oranges.

Praise be to you, Lord. I have never tasted anything as wonderful in my entire life.

Having been on the Island of Despair, as I called it, for one year, I knew when the dry season and the wet season were. I sowed about two-thirds of my grain during the dry season, and it yielded nothing.

But I had better luck when I planted in February, as I could take advantage of the heavy rains.

When there was time, I explored my island further.

Land, old man! Fifteen, maybe, twenty leagues away. Perhaps I am not so far from civilisation as I first thought.

But which civilisation can it be? Could be the Americans. Could be the Spanish.

Or the cannibals.

I went back to exploring the island and put the foreign land out of my mind for some time.

After spending hours exploring the island, my dog and I walked back home and, on our way, made a new friend – Poll, the parrot.

SKRAWWWKK

By then it was 30th September 1661, and I had been on the island for two years – two years of being a prisoner, trapped there by the ocean that stretched out as far as I could see.

At times I thought I would never be able to leave the place.

To soothe myself, I read the *Holy Bible* daily, and trusted in my faith – God had not forsaken me.

'I will never, never leave thee, nor forsake thee.'

Then there were days when I did not have time to dwell on my situation. After all, surviving was an all-consuming task, and that meant protecting my food supply.

It has taken me three weeks to make this fence. Now the corn can grow strong and safe.

These words were for me. Why else should they be directed in such a manner, just at the moment when I was mourning over my condition?

Good work, old man! We cannot afford to share our food with the wild animals.

GGRRR RUFF

When it rained and I was housebound, I tried to teach Poll to speak.

Pretty Polly!

And I continued to experiment to make my life more comfortable – this time by making pots!

WOOF WOOF

THUD!

Stand back! This could get messy.

It is hard to tell how many awkward ways I tried to raise the paste; and the odd, ugly things I made. So many pots fell in and others fell out because the clay was not stiff enough to bear its own weight. Others being set out in the sun too hastily, fell into pieces.

My next concern was to get a stone mortar, to stamp or beat some corn in. This would allow me to make bread.

♫ I knew me a fine gal, lived in London town. When last went ashore, she showed me around. Had me a grand time, with this little miss. All went well, till I stole me a kiss! ♫

Though I miscarried so much in my design for large pots, yet I made several other things with better success; and the heat of the sun baked them quite hard.

After weeks of hard work, the mortar was ready, and soon after the bread.

This is the best bread I have ever tasted!

I always kept myself busy, but whenever I was free, my thoughts ran upon the land which I had seen from the other side of the island. While I wished I was on its shores, I was aware of the dangers of going there.

I have heard that the people of the Caribbean coast are cannibals and, based on our latitude, we could not be far from that shore.

But I had made up my mind to leave the island. One day I went searching for the boat from my ship and found it...

I need to... ugh...get off this island... oooof...

...but this lifeboat is too heavy to launch in the water.

We need to leave this place, but we do not have a boat that is of any use to us.

This started me thinking...

...was it not possible to make myself a canoe?

Time passed. My clothes were beginning to wear off and I needed a new suit. There was nobody around to mind my nudity...

...but my body could not stand the rays of the sun without protection. And the sun was so strong that I needed a hat before leaving my house.

Therefore, I made myself some clothes and a cap from the skins of all the creatures that I had killed till then. After that, I spent a great deal of time and effort making an umbrella.

For the next five years, nothing extraordinary happened to me. I continued to live on in the same manner, just as before.

The chief thing that kept me busy, besides tending my crops, was making a new canoe.

When it was ready, I dug a canal six-feet wide, and four-feet deep; and brought it into the creek, a distance of almost half-a-mile.

Then I went on a tour round the island.

The discoveries I made in that little journey made me very eager to see other parts of the coast. So, every morning I would leave on my boat to look around.

As time passed, I began to realise that my gunpowder was running low, and it was impossible for me to replace it. I seriously began to consider what I would do when there was none left.

In the eleventh year of my residence on the island, I decided to find a way to trap and snare the goats.

I resolved to dig several large pits in the earth, where I had observed the goats feeding. If I expected to supply myself with goat flesh when I had no powder left, taming them was my only way.

Life went on, and I had started thinking that I was the prince and lord of the whole island...

...when my belief was shattered!

One day at about noon, I saw the print of a man's naked foot on the shore. I went up and down the beach, but could not see another impression except that one.

I went back to it to confirm that I had not imagined it, but there was no doubt about it. It was the print of a foot — complete with toes, heel and every part of a foot. How it got there, I did not know, nor could I imagine.

I could not sleep that night. The farther I was from the footprint, the greater my apprehensions were... which seemed contrary to the nature of fear.

I thought it must be the Devil. But it would be strange for Satan to take human form in such a place, and then only leave a footprint behind!

I decided it must be some of the savages from the mainland who had wandered out to sea in their canoes.

I was thankful that I had not been there at that time and that they had not seen my boat. If they had, they would have concluded that some inhabitants had been there and, perhaps, would have searched for me.

I did not leave my castle for three days and nights, but then I began to run out of provisions. Also, I knew my goats needed to be milked.

One day it came into my mind that all that might have been a figment of my imagination; and the footprint could have been my own! I heartened myself with that belief and began to venture out again.

Over the next few years, I took all the measures I could think of, to ensure undetected survival.

One day, while wandering along the west point of the island, I saw a boat at a great distance. I ran down the hill.

As I was going down, I realised that seeing the print of a man's foot on the island was not such a strange thing...

...because but what I saw next left me speechless!

The shore was covered with skulls, hands, feet and other bones of human bodies.

Heavenly Father! No!

I turned my face away from the horrid spectacle. My stomach felt sick and I vomited with an uncommon violence.

I also observed that a fire had been made, and a circle dug in the earth, where the savages must have sat down to their inhuman feasting upon the bodies of their fellow creatures.

I could not bear to stay there any longer, so I ran back up the hill as fast as I could, and went towards my home.

I thanked God that fate had landed me in that part of the world where I was free from such dreadful creatures as these cannibals.

I might be here for eighteen more years if they do not discover me. My only business is to keep myself entirely concealed.

I had been there almost eighteen years and had observed that those savages never came to the island in search of anything. Perhaps they expected nothing to be there.

I kept close within my own circle for the next two years and I never fired my gun off once. However, I always carried the three pistols, that I had saved from the ship, with me.

No mater how hard I would try to not think about them, my thoughts would wander towards those savages.

Some days all I could think of was how I could destroy those monsters and, if possible, save the victim they might take there to kill.

I made my tour every morning up to the top of the hill to see if I could observe any boats coming near the island. As time passed, my resolve to do these creatures harm wore down.

Lord, what right do I have to kill these savages? If you do not see fit to punish them for their actions, how can I justify doing it?

If I wrote down all the ways I imagined destroying these creatures, it would be larger than the whole of this work.

These people had done me no injury. If they attempted to harm me, then it could be justified, but they had no knowledge of me. Therefore, it would not be right to attack them.

I started living a retired life, and seldom left my cell, other than to milk my goats and manage my little flock in the wood. But these were on the other side of the island and quite out of danger.

Time passed. In my twenty-third year on the island, I found a deep, natural cave where, I believe, no savage had been.

Its floor is dry and level. I should keep my magazine of powder and spare arms here.

It was the month of December when, before daylight, I was surprised to see the light of a fire upon the shore.

It was about two miles away, towards the end of the island, where I had seen some savages before.

But they were not on the other side... they were on my side of the island!

49

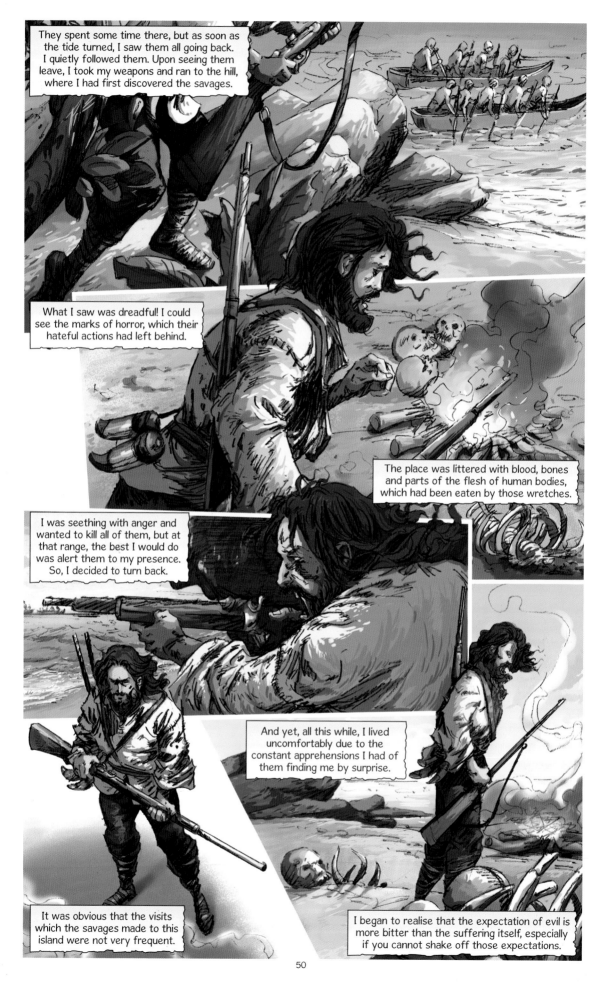

They spent some time there, but as soon as the tide turned, I saw them all going back. I quietly followed them. Upon seeing them leave, I took my weapons and ran to the hill, where I had first discovered the savages.

What I saw was dreadful! I could see the marks of horror, which their hateful actions had left behind.

The place was littered with blood, bones and parts of the flesh of human bodies, which had been eaten by those wretches.

I was seething with anger and wanted to kill all of them, but at that range, the best I would do was alert them to my presence. So, I decided to turn back.

And yet, all this while, I lived uncomfortably due to the constant apprehensions I had of them finding me by surprise.

It was obvious that the visits which the savages made to this island were not very frequent.

I began to realise that the expectation of evil is more bitter than the suffering itself, especially if you cannot shake off those expectations.

A year and three months passed before I saw the savages again. Meanwhile, in the middle of May, I experienced a very great storm with a great deal of lightning and thunder.

KA-POW

KA-BAM

Lord, please do not let my mind play tricks on me. Send me another sign that civilised men are nearby.

I do not know exactly when it was but, one day, I was surprised by what I thought was the noise of gunfire at sea.

I assumed that it must be a ship in distress, and that they had another ship with them who had fired the guns to obtain help.

Then I realised that though I could not help them, they could be of help to me. I brought together all the dry wood I could get and, making a pile, I set it on fire upon the hill.

I tended my fire all night until day broke. When it was broad day, I saw the wreck of a ship cast away upon some concealed rocks.

Desperate for supplies, and hoping for a companion, I set sail towards the ship.

The fate of those who had been on board gave me more and more reason to thank God, who had provided for me in my desolate condition.

As for the dead, I could do no more than look upon the misery of these poor men, and pity them.

Hello! Is anyone here?

I wished that there had been one soul saved from this ship, so that I might have had a companion.

Throughout my life, I had never felt so desperate. The desire to belong to a society with my fellow men was so strong and the regret at the impossibility of this so deep!

Anyone at all. Please, answer me.

In the staterooms, I found some items that had survived the storm, including some rum, a fire shovel and tongs, brass kettles, and a grid iron.

Most importantly, I discovered a powder horn with four pounds of powder.

Upon further examination, I also found several shirts, handkerchiefs and neckcloths that were most welcomed. I resolved to store these goods in my cave and not carry them home.

Of all the things I could have found on the ship, money was of the least concern to me.

Ironically, one of the chests that had not been touched by water contained several hundred coins and gold bars worth thousands of pounds.

SLAM

CHINK...CLINK

I got what I could on the island, and life went on as usual.

I spent the next two years thinking of ways to escape. One night I was wondering what might happen if I reached the island I had seen from the hill top, when I drifted off to sleep. It was then that I had a strange dream...

...I saw cannibals approaching my island – their intent full of pure malice.

There was a man who looked like the cannibals, but he was not one of them. Rather, he was one of their intended victims.

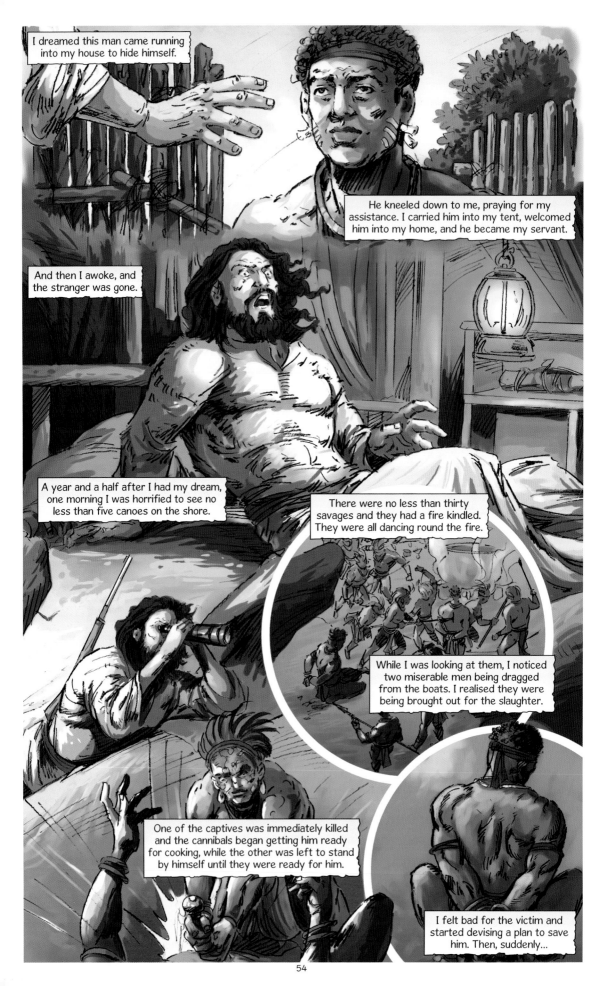

...the victim saw his chance for liberty. Inspired by the hope of survival, he broke away from the savages.

I was dreadfully frightened when I saw him coming in my direction, especially when I saw the entire band of savages chasing after him.

I saw that he was running directly towards me and towards the part of the island where my habitation was.

SPLASH

I expected my dream to come true – that this man would seek shelter in my grove.

WHIZZZ

I saw only three men chasing this fellow which relieved me to an extent.

KA-POW

I knew that it was time to save that man's life, and perhaps get myself a companion.

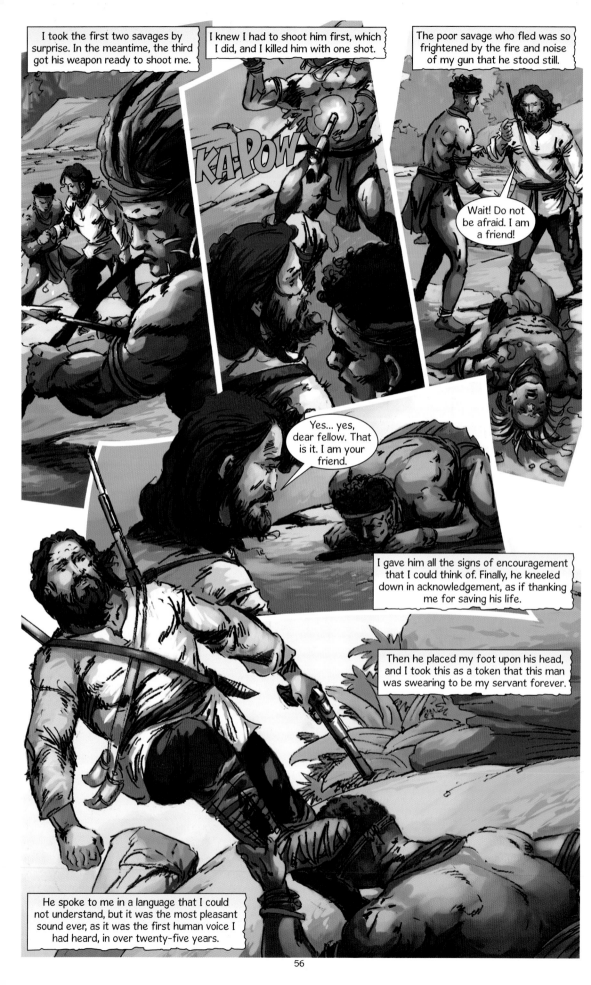

I took the first two savages by surprise. In the meantime, the third got his weapon ready to shoot me.

I knew I had to shoot him first, which I did, and I killed him with one shot.

The poor savage who fled was so frightened by the fire and noise of my gun that he stood still.

Wait! Do not be afraid. I am a friend!

Yes... yes, dear fellow. That is it. I am your friend.

I gave him all the signs of encouragement that I could think of. Finally, he kneeled down in acknowledgement, as if thanking me for saving his life.

Then he placed my foot upon his head, and I took this as a token that this man was swearing to be my servant forever.

He spoke to me in a language that I could not understand, but it was the most pleasant sound ever, as it was the first human voice I had heard, in over twenty-five years.

KA-POW

No man had ever had a more faithful, loving, sincere servant than Friday was to me. He was extremely helpful and was interested in learning. He showed me great friendship and, I believe, he would have sacrificed his life for mine.

Friday was the most able scholar, and in a little while, began to talk very well. I soon learned that he and the others had been political prisoners, who were going to be put to death for supporting their old king.

Friday... master...

I taught him everything that he needed to know to make him useful, handy and helpful. I also taught him my language so that it was easier to communicate with him.

I trusted Friday so much that I decided to teach him how to hunt with the musket...

God preserve!

KAPOW

Initially, when I fired the weapon in his presence, he thought I was going to kill him.

Oh, master. Please strike me not dead!

Friday! Off your knees. And go fetch the carcass.

Thankfully, Friday soon got over this fear and became quite a good shot himself.

Then I taught him how to make bread, plant corn and, most importantly... how to enjoy the taste of cooked animal flesh!

Some time later, Friday and I were at the top of the hill on the east side of the island. The weather was serene, and Friday called out to me in surprise.

Oh, joy! Oh, glad! There see my country. There my nation.

If only I could go home, Master Crusoe.

I noticed an extraordinary sense of pleasure appear on Friday's face. He suddenly became excited, as if he wanted to be in his own country again.

What if I could make a canoe to send you home, Friday? What would you do?

Friday, tell me, what would you do if you returned to your country? Would you turn wild again? Would you forget the true God and eat men's flesh again?

I would go, if you go with me.

Friday, come with me. I need to share something with you.

I took Friday to where my boat had been all these years. We found that the sun had dried and split it, and it was rotten. I told Friday we would make another boat as big as that one and go home in it.

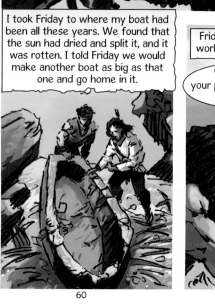

No, I tell my people live good. Tell them to pray to God.

Friday and I went to work making a canoe.

What about your people? Will they eat me?

No! Me make sure they no eat you. Me make sure they much love you.

Would he tell his countrymen about me and come back with a hundred of them to make a feast out of me?

After aout a month's hard labour, the boat was ready.

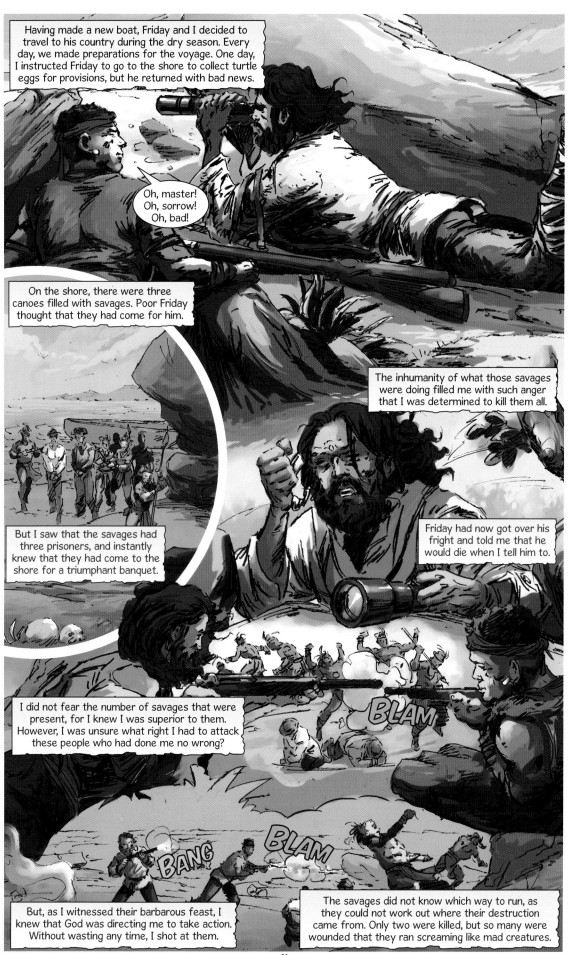

Having made a new boat, Friday and I decided to travel to his country during the dry season. Every day, we made preparations for the voyage. One day, I instructed Friday to go to the shore to collect turtle eggs for provisions, but he returned with bad news.

Oh, master!
Oh, sorrow!
Oh, bad!

On the shore, there were three canoes filled with savages. Poor Friday thought that they had come for him.

The inhumanity of what those savages were doing filled me with such anger that I was determined to kill them all.

But I saw that the savages had three prisoners, and instantly knew that they had come to the shore for a triumphant banquet.

Friday had now got over his fright and told me that he would die when I tell him to.

I did not fear the number of savages that were present, for I knew I was superior to them. However, I was unsure what right I had to attack these people who had done me no wrong?

BLAM

BANG

BLAM

But, as I witnessed their barbarous feast, I knew that God was directing me to take action. Without wasting any time, I shot at them.

The savages did not know which way to run, as they could not work out where their destruction came from. Only two were killed, but so many were wounded that they ran screaming like mad creatures.

I went directly towards the poor victim where the butchers had left him. I questioned this man.

Where are you from, friend?

Spain.

A Spaniard? We will talk afterwards, but now we must fight!

As I pulled the Spaniard to safety, Friday was surprised to find another poor creature lying in one of the canoes. His hands and feet were tied and he was ready for the slaughter. The man was almost dead with fear and did not know what had happened.

Friday peeped inside and...

...upon seeing the man, he cried, laughed, jumped about and danced.

When he calmed down, he told me that the man was his father.

I took the prisoners to my house, and boiled a stew of goat meat, barley and rice.

As we ate, I wondered if the natives might return. Friday's father felt that they would be so frightened by the way they were attacked that they would not come back.

Then I turned to the Spaniard.

There are sixteen more Spaniards and Portuguese, who had been cast away. They are trapped there as they have no powder for weapons. They are helpless!

I swear to not move till you give me orders. I will take your side to the last drop of my blood, if my countrymen break my word.

I will help your countrymen if you vow not to turn on me.

Taking the Spaniard's advice, we decided to wait half a year before rescuing his comrades. In the meantime, I set to make sure my stock of corn and rice was sufficient for us and all of them.

I also set about increasing the size of my flock in anticipation of the new arrivals.

At last, when all was ready, the Spaniard and Friday's father went away in one of the canoes that they had been brought in as prisoners.

We had been waiting for them for almost eight days when a strange incident took place.

Master, they are come, they are come!

When I looked out to sea, I was surprised to see a boat some miles from us. I observed that a fairly strong wind was bringing them in.

I fetched my perspective glass and discovered an anchored ship.

It appeared to be an English ship.

I was very confused but I must admit that the joy of seeing a ship – and one manned by my own countrymen – was overwhelming.

I was happy, but I had some secret doubts which kept me on my guard.

63

We went closer and found that there were aroud ten men on the shore, three of whom were prisoners.

Oh, master! You see English mans eat prisoner as well as savage mans.

No, Friday. I am afraid they will murder them, but you can be sure they will not eat them.

Do not be surprised to see me, gentlemen. Perhaps, you have a friend near you when you least expect it.

Am I talking to God or man?

In the afternoon, I noticed that the sailors had all gone wandering into the woods and had lain down to sleep.

The three poor distressed prisoners were too anxious to get any sleep. They had been left about a quarter of a mile from me and were out of sight of any of the others.

I am an Englishman, and am here to assist you. Come with me.

As we returned to my camp, I discovered that I had rescued the ship's commander, whose crew had mutinied against him. The two other men were his first mate and a passenger.

Your murderers are asleep, Captain. You will have my help in killing or capturing them, whichever you like.

I do not want to kill all of them. There are two villains among them. If they are secured, I believe the rest would return to duty.

I will help you, and all I ask in return is that you will carry me and my man to England for free.

The ship and I shall be directed and commanded by you for this service.

The captain was hesitant to take up arms against these men but, during our conversation, we heard the mutineers awake. I had no choice... so, I shot at the men.

BANG

BANG

Two of them made some noise, and one of the seamen cried out to the rest.

One of the villains was killed on the spot and the other wounded. As for the other mutineers...

I will spare your lives if you swear to be faithful to me in recovering the ship, and carrying her back to Jamaica.

I do!

I sent Friday with the captain's mate to the boat with orders to secure her.

Our victory was complete.

Thank you, Mr Crusoe, but what about the ship?

I am thinking of a way to take control without the men causing much trouble.

KA-BAM

KA-BAM

But how do you plan--

The gunfire is not a good sign! The mutineers want the men to return to the ship.

Captain, I have a plan to get your command back.

65

I told him the plan and he agreed. He set on the boat with the mutineers and moved towards the ship. He manned his boat in a very competent way. As soon as he came close to the ship, he got one of the mutineers to hail them.

The captain entered first, with his arms at the ready, followed by his mate.

Being very well supported by their men, they secured all those on deck. Then they began to fasten the hatches, to ensure that anyone who was below would stay there.

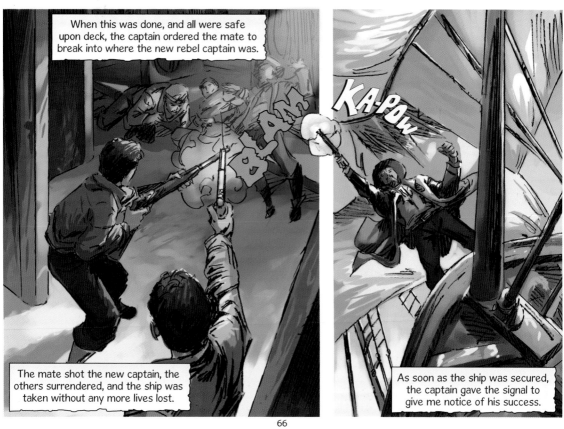

When this was done, and all were safe upon deck, the captain ordered the mate to break into where the new rebel captain was.

The mate shot the new captain, the others surrendered, and the ship was taken without any more lives lost.

As soon as the ship was secured, the captain gave the signal to give me notice of his success.

My sentence was at an end.

Oh, for joy, master! For much joy!

Indeed. Much joy.

When he come back, the captain and I began to consult on what was to be done with the prisoners.

If I carry them away, they must be delivered to justice at the first English colony we come to.

For your mutinous act, you would face the gallows should you return home. But, if you would prefer to try your luck on the island, then you are free to do so.

I had another idea.

I suggest you all rather stay here than return to England to be hanged.

The Spaniard and his comrades will be returning soon. Treat them well.

Having left instructions with the mutineers, I boarded the ship the next day. Once on board, I wasted no time in shaving my beard. We then prepared to sail for home immediately.

When I finally left my island, I took few souvenirs with me. I had my goat skin cap, umbrella and the money I had recovered from my ship and the Spanish vessel.

I also had my servant and friend, Friday, by my side. I had returned a very wealthy man but, more importantly, I returned a wiser man.

I left my island on 19th December 1686 and arrived home on 11th June 1687 after an absence of thirty-five years. When I returned to England, I was a perfect stranger to all the world, as if I had never been known there.

But unlike the boy I was when I left, I now knew who I was and what type of man I was to be. I finally knew my place in the world.

The End

CAMPFIRE™

About Us

It is night-time in the forest. The sky is black, studded with countless stars. A campfire is crackling, and the storytelling has begun. Stories about love and wisdom, conflict and power, dreams and identity, courage and adventure, survival against all odds, and hope against all hope – they have all come to the fore in a stream of words, gestures, song and dance. The warm, cheerful radiance of the campfire has awoken the storyteller in all those present. Even the trees and the earth and the animals of the forest seem to have fallen silent, captivated, bewitched.

Inspired by this enduring relationship between a campfire and the stories it evokes, we began publishing under the Campfire imprint in 2008, with the vision of creating graphic novels of the finest quality to entertain and educate our readers. Our writers, editors, artists and colourists share a deep passion for good stories and the art of storytelling, so our books are well researched, beautifully illustrated and wonderfully written to create a most enjoyable reading experience.

Our graphic novels are presently being published in four exciting categories. The *Classics* category showcases popular and timeless literature, which has been faithfully adapted for today's readers. While these adaptations retain the flavour of the era, they encourage our readers to delve into the literary world with the aid of authentic graphics and simplified language. Titles in the *Originals* category feature imaginative new characters and intriguing plots, and will be highly anticipated and appreciated by lovers of fiction. Our *Mythology* titles tap into the vast library of epics, myths, and legends from India and abroad, not just presenting tales from time immemorial, but also addressing their modern-day relevance. And our *Biography* titles explore the life and times of eminent personalities from around the world, in a manner that is both inspirational and personal.

Crafted by a new generation of talented artists and writers, all our graphic novels boast cutting-edge artwork, an engaging narrative, and have universal and lasting appeal.

Whether you are an avid reader or an occasional one, we hope you will gather around our campfire and let us draw you into our fascinating world of storytelling.

FIVE FAMOUS SHIPWRECKS

MARY ROSE

Once described by Henry VIII as 'the fairest flower of all the ships that ever sailed', the *Mary Rose* took two years to build and was fitted with a 'broadside'. This meant that its cannons were placed on one side of the ship, providing devastating fire power against enemy vessels. On 19th July 1545, the *Mary Rose* keeled over as it sailed out to engage French ships in battle. An exact explanation of why the ship sank has yet to be found, but it is thought that over 600 crew members died that day. When the *Mary Rose* wreck was lifted from the sea in 1982, the event was captured by television cameras and watched by an estimated 60 million viewers.

TITANIC

The *Titanic* was the most extravagant passenger liner of her era, meant to be completely unsinkable. Wealthy travellers could enjoy the use of an on-board swimming pool, an extensive library, a gym, and a Turkish bath. After colliding with an iceberg on 15th April 1912, the *Titanic* sank into the North Atlantic Ocean on its maiden voyage from Southampton to New York. The resting place of the *Titanic* is 2.5 miles underwater.
There were suggestions of a *Titanic* curse due to the presence of the mummy of Princess of Amen-Ra on board. The owner of the mummy took it onto the ship hidden under his car to avoid causing a panic among the passengers.

There are striking similarities between the novel *Futility* by MF Mansfield with the real-life story of the *Titanic*. The amazing fact is that the novel was first published in 1898 – fourteen years before the *Titanic* sank!!

LUSITANIA

Built to be a British passenger liner, the *Lusitania* was handed over to the British Admiralty and equipped with twelve 6-inch guns in August 1914. This was due to the outbreak of the First World War. A German embassy later issued a warning notice in American newspapers to travellers. It stated that a war existed between Germany and Britain, and that the waters adjacent to the British Isles were considered a war zone. It stated that travellers sailing there do so at their own risk. On Friday, 9th May 1915, the *Lusitania* was sunk by a torpedo from a U20 German submarine. One of the casualties was Justus Miles Forman, an American novelist and playwright. It is strange that days before he embarked on the *Lusitania* voyage, he received a mysterious phone call which warned him not to board the *Lusitania*.

BISMARCK

An intimidating German warship, the *Bismarck* had a displacement of 50,000 tons, a top speed of 30 knots, and was 17-storeys high and over 800-feet long. During the Second World War, the British Prime Minister, Winston Churchill, gave orders for the *Bismarck* to be sunk on sight. In May 1941, the *Bismarck* was chased by the British navy for 8 days. Faced with such a bombardment, the ship was heavily damaged, and sank. In 1989, after searching an area of 200 square miles, Dr Robert D Ballard found the wreck of the *Bismarck* – it was more than 15,000 feet beneath the surface of the Atlantic!

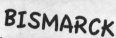

BELGRANO

On 2nd May 1982, an Argentine Navy cruiser known as the *Belgrano* was attacked by *HMS Conqueror*, the British nuclear submarine. Three torpedoes were fired at the Argentine warship, which sank as a result of the damage. The *Belgrano* had previously been an American ship which had survived the Japanese attack on Pearl Harbour during the Second World War. The ship was sold to Argentina during the 1950s. In 2003, a film company attempted to search for the ship using a remote-controlled submersible, and sonar equipment. The crew did not manage to find the wreck, which is thought to be 180 kilometres off the coast of Argentina, known for its dangerous seas.

Available now

Putting the fun back into reading!